FATHER CHRISTMAS

Other books by Raymond Briggs

FATHER CHRISTMAS GOES ON HOLIDAY
JIM AND THE BEANSTALK
FUNGUS THE BOGEYMAN
THE SNOWMAN
THE SNOWMAN STORY BOOK

RAYMOND BRIGGS
Father Christmas

PUFFIN BOOKS

For my Mother and Father

PUFFIN BOOKS

Published by the Penguin Group
Penguin Books Ltd, 80 Strand, London WC2R 0RL, England
Penguin Putnam Inc., 375 Hudson Street, New York, New York 10014, USA
Penguin Books Australia Ltd, 250 Camberwell Road, Camberwell, Victoria 3124, Australia
Penguin Books Canada Ltd, 10 Alcorn Avenue, Toronto, Ontario, Canada M4V 3B2
Penguin Books India (P) Ltd, 11 Community Centre, Panchsheel Park, New Delhi – 110 017, India
Penguin Books (NZ) Ltd, Cnr Rosedale and Airborne Roads, Albany, Auckland, New Zealand
Penguin Books (South Africa) (Pty) Ltd, 24 Sturdee Avenue, Rosebank 2196, South Africa

Penguin Books Ltd, Registered Offices: 80 Strand, London WC2R 0RL, England

www.penguin.com

First published in Great Britain by Hamish Hamilton 1973
First published in the United States of America by Coward, McCann, & Geoghegan 1973
Published in Picture Puffins 1974
35 37 39 40 38 36 34

Copyright © Raymond Briggs, 1973
All rights reserved

Made and printed in Italy by Printer Trento Srl

British Library Cataloguing in Publication Data
A CIP catalogue record for this book is available from the British Library

0–140–50125–8

Father Christmas

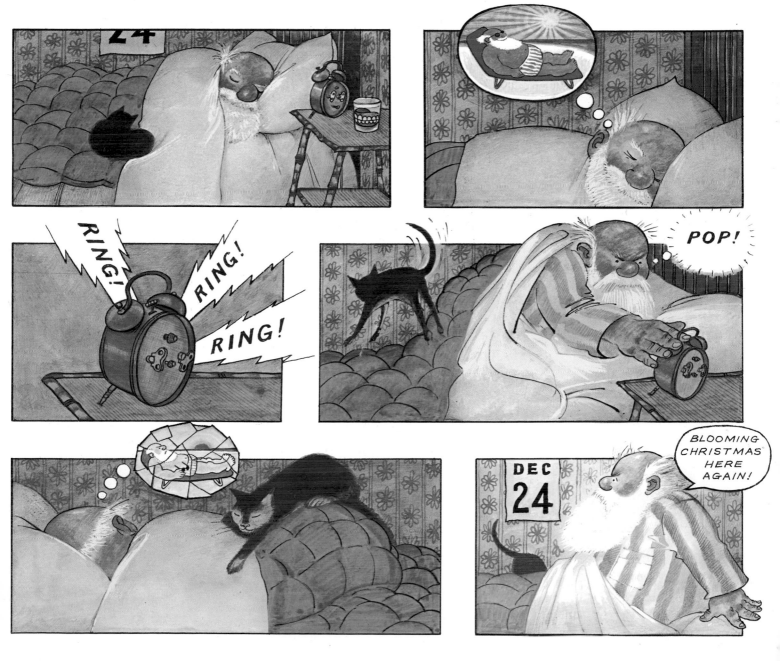

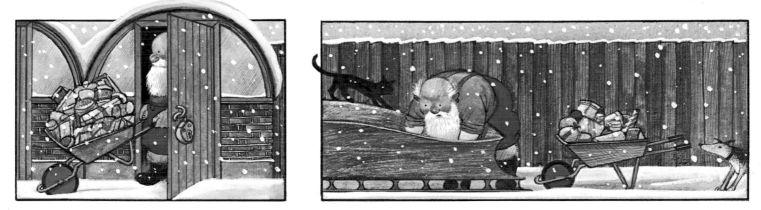

KEEP STILL YOU SILLY DEERS!

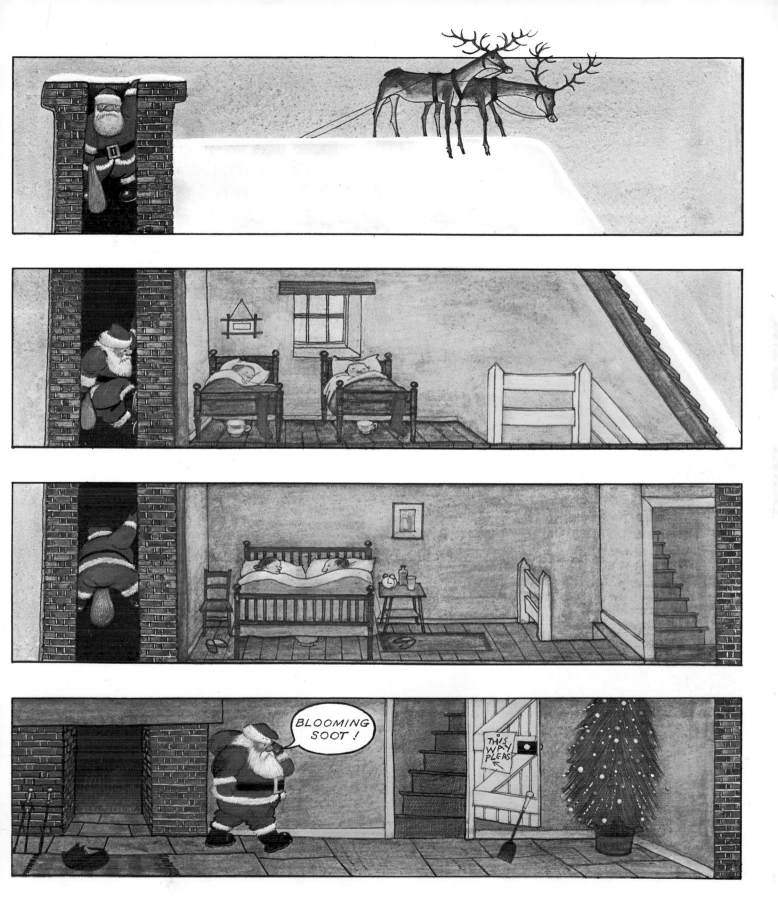

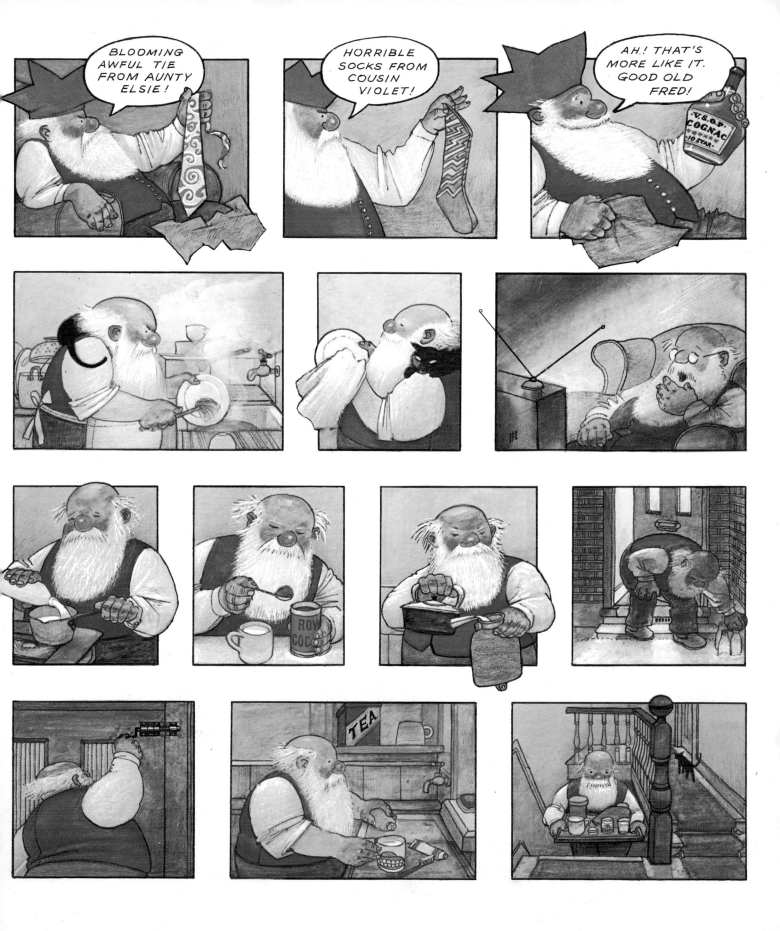

The End